SP21 cut

Ideal for

We hope yo_____is book
Ple_____ _____ __e date.
_

Full of
Christmassy
magic

Beautiful
illustrations
that will really get
you in the festive
spirit

Lucy
helps a puppy
find his
forever home

Make
a wish!

Here's the moment that
Lucy meets Boots the puppy
for the first time...

Lucy rang the doorbell, and Gran opened the door—but instead of giving Lucy a hug she had her arms full of a squirmy, waggy, adorable puppy.

'Gran! Where did you get such a gorgeous puppy?' exclaimed Lucy in delight, as she put all her bags down and went to give her gran a hug. The puppy launched itself into her arms and covered her face with licks. Lucy held it tightly and felt its soft puppy fur. It was so warm, with a special baby animal scent which made Lucy's heart melt.

LUCY MAKES
A WISH

Written by
Anne Booth

Illustrated by
Sophy Williams

OXFORD
UNIVERSITY PRESS

OXFORD
UNIVERSITY PRESS

Great Clarendon Street, Oxford OX2 6DP

Oxford University Press is a department of the University of Oxford.
It furthers the University's objective of excellence in research, scholarship,
and education by publishing worldwide. Oxford is a registered trade mark of
Oxford University Press in the UK and in certain other countries

British Library Cataloguing in Publication Data
Data available

ISBN: 978-0-19-277248-0

1 3 5 7 9 10 8 6 4 2

Printed in Great Britain

Paper used in the production of this book is a natural,
recyclable product made from wood grown in sustainable forests.
The manufacturing process conforms to the environmental
regulations of the country of origin.

To
Jossie and Dougie

Chapter One

It was the end of the last day of school, the Christmas holidays were about to begin, and Lucy was feeling very happy. The last few days had been lots of fun, with no more homework, a special Christmas dinner, a concert, and even a pantomime where the teachers dressed up. Today all the staff were wearing Christmas jumpers and everyone was making Christmas decorations. The classroom was festooned with brightly coloured paper chains and paper snowflakes. Lucy loved being at school, but she was ready for the term to end. Christmas holidays always seemed to be especially magical for Lucy.

'I can't wait to be on holiday!' Lucy said to Rosie, her best friend.

'Neither can I!' said Rosie. 'Do you want to meet up tomorrow?'

'That would be fun,' said Lucy.

'I've promised Gran to help give the Rescue Centre a good clean in the morning, but I could come in the afternoon? I can come over next week and help you with the donkeys then, too.' Lucy smiled happily. It was so great that her gran had a wildlife rescue centre, and her best friend's family ran a donkey sanctuary and farm. Lucy loved animals so much, and she wanted to be a vet when she grew up.

'We're a bit worried about our latest rescue donkey,' said Rosie. 'She isn't eating and she's so sad all the time, and she won't even go near Pixie and Elf.'

Lucy noticed Alfie, the new boy in the class, looking over at them. Alfie was very shy, and Lucy thought this might be a good time to make friends with him, but when she turned back to talk to him he was concentrating on the decoration he was making. Lucy saw it was a silhouette of a reindeer in white card.

'That's so good!' said Lucy, admiringly, but Alfie just went a bit red, and then the bell went for the end of school.

'Happy Christmas everyone! See you in January!' said Miss Brown.

'See you tomorrow!' said Rosie, giving Lucy a hug. Her little sister Leah was waiting outside with their mum, and jumping up and down. Lucy waved at them through the window and turned to say happy Christmas to Alfie, but he had gone already.

School had closed early, but Mum and Dad were still at work, and her brother Oscar was away on a school trip. Gran said that, as it was the last day at school, and Lucy would have things to carry home, she was going to come over to Lucy's house before Lucy got home and make her a special end of term cake for tea. Lucy rang the doorbell, and Gran opened the door—but instead of giving

Lucy a hug she had her arms full of a squirmy, waggy, adorable puppy.

'Gran! Where did you get such a gorgeous puppy?' exclaimed Lucy in delight, as she put all her bags down and went to give her gran a hug. The puppy launched itself into her arms and covered her face with licks. Lucy held it tightly and felt its soft puppy fur. It was so warm, with a special baby animal scent which made Lucy's heart melt. For a minute Lucy let herself hope that it might be Gran's present to her, but it wasn't Christmas yet, and Lucy knew her family had decided not to have a dog, as both her parents worked and she and

Oscar were out at school all day.

'Well, my lovely neighbour Eva had only had him for a couple of weeks when she had to go and stay with her mother who was very ill, so she asked me to look after little Boots yesterday. The trouble is, she rang me today and she has a big problem. Her mother is getting better, but Eva has decided she should move up there to look after her, and her mother is allergic to dogs. I wasn't expecting to suddenly have a puppy to look after as well as all the other animals!'

'Are you going to keep him, Gran?' said Lucy, hopefully. 'I'll help!'

'I don't think it would be fair on him,

Lucy,' said Gran. 'I've got the energy to look after sick hedgehogs and small mammals and birds, but I don't think I have time for the long walks he will need, and my garden just isn't big enough. I'll keep him over Christmas, and then when it's the New Year we'll look for a lovely new home for him. One where he can have lots of exercise and won't be bored. Oh dear!'

Boots had jumped out of Lucy's arms and onto the sofa where he was wrestling with a cushion.

'I'm glad we haven't put the tree up yet!' laughed Lucy. 'Imagine Boots with one!'

'I remember when Merry was a kitten—she thought it was fun to climb to the top!' said Gran, smiling. 'I haven't seen her since I came. She seems to be keeping out of the way with Boots.'

Boots did not want to leave the

cushion, but Gran enticed him down with a soft toy in the shape of a cow, and while Gran went into the kitchen to cut Lucy a slice of a chocolate cake she had made, Lucy took some more dog toys out of a little basket Gran had brought, and threw them around the room for Boots to chase. The little puppy scampered enthusiastically around, his tail wagging. Then suddenly, he flopped on the floor next to Lucy, wagged his tail again, gave her sock a lick and fell fast asleep.

'That's one thing about puppies,' laughed Gran, as she came in with the cake and tea. 'They do sleep a great deal of the day!'

Lucy washed her hands and sat down next to Gran to eat the delicious cake.

'I wonder if Rosie could take him?' said Lucy, hopefully. 'There are lots of fields nearby—lots of people take their dogs for walks there.'

'I rang Rosie's mum and asked her, but she said that they were so busy with the donkeys and setting up the sanctuary café at the moment, that she didn't think it was good timing.'

'Well, I'll definitely help with him, Gran,' said Lucy.

Boots opened his eyes and yawned.

'Quick, Lucy!' laughed Gran. 'He is waking up! We need to get him outside in the garden before there is a puddle on your mum and dad's floor!' Lucy scooped the surprised puppy up and took him out into the garden. He was very interested in sniffing everything, and ran around, his nose to the ground, his tail wagging, then did a wee.

'He is actually very good for a young puppy,' said Gran, as they stood watching him happily explore, 'and I am relieved to say he slept through the night without accidents, but he still needs house-training.'

'I can spend every day with him over the holidays,' said Lucy. 'I'd love to get experience with a puppy, and maybe I can even teach him tricks!'

'If you can just train him not to chew up everything in sight that would be a help,' sighed Gran. 'He is so intelligent, and he is into mischief of all kinds, but you can't help but love him!'

As if he heard them, Boots rushed up, wagging his tail, with a plastic flowerpot in his mouth. Gran persuaded him to give it up by swapping a treat for it, and then they went inside. Lucy played some more with him, throwing balls, and then she had him on her lap as she watched some television. He tried to chew her jumper, so she gave him a squeaky bone to play with, which he loved. What a great holiday this was turning out to be!

Mum and Dad both came home together, made a fuss of Boots, and then Gran took him home. Dad cooked a curry, with poppadums and naan bread, and they finished off the yummy chocolate cake Gran had made together.

'Shall we get the tree tomorrow, Lucy?' said Dad.

'I've got to go over to Gran's and help look after Boots, but I suppose we could bring him with us after lunch?' said Lucy.

'Good idea—that will take some pressure off Gran,' said Dad.

'And do you think I could take him shopping with us too? I've just remembered I'm going with Rosie in the afternoon.'

'I know puppies need to get lots of experience when they are young, so that might be good for him, but you won't be able to take him into all the shops,' said Mum. 'Maybe we should get some advice from Gran or Nieve the vet.'

Lucy said goodnight to her mum and dad and went up to bed to read her puppy book. She loved her cosy bedroom. On her bed lay Scruffy the pyjama-case dog and Mistletoe the donkey, and beside the bed was Rocky, an old rocking horse with the kindest expression in his eyes. He always seemed as if he was listening to her.

'I know it wouldn't be fair to have a puppy when nobody is at home in the day, but Boots is so sweet, I do wish we could keep him,' said Lucy, a bit sadly to Rocky as she got ready for bed. As she said it, the not quite closed door was pushed open, and her beautiful ginger cat Merry walked into the room. She padded over to Lucy and rubbed herself against her legs, and then gave a graceful leap onto the bed, purring loudly as she settled down.

'At least I've got the best cat in the

world,' said Lucy. Merry kept her position on the bedclothes, still purring, as Lucy carefully got in. 'It will be a very interesting holiday looking after a puppy,' she said, 'and maybe I can help Gran find a good family for him. It's a shame Rosie's family can't take him—I'd see him often if they did.' She yawned, almost as widely as little Boots had earlier, and looked over at her snow globe on the side table. She leant over and picked it up.

'You always seem to be especially sparkly at Christmas,' Lucy said, as she shook it. She watched the snowflakes whirl around the glass globe, falling onto a little house in the woods. 'I'll take

Boots to the woods tomorrow when we
go and get the tree. I wish that we could
find the perfect family for him,' she said,
sleepily, and put the globe back on the

table. Suddenly the snow globe started glowing. The snowflakes turned from white to silver and then all the colours of the rainbow as they whirled faster and faster around the globe.

Lucy got a lovely warm, magical feeling inside her tummy as she looked over at the globe. Happiness tingled and spread from her toes up to her head.

'Oh Boots, this Christmas with you is going to be magical, I just know it! I can't wait for tomorrow to see you again,' she said, just before she fell fast asleep.

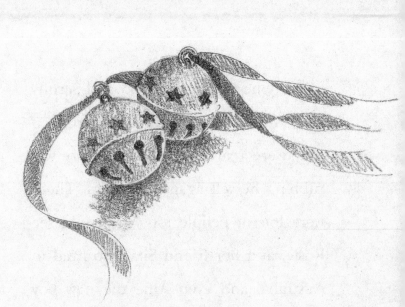

Chapter Two

Lucy had such a lovely dream, filled with all the animals she and Gran had helped. There were rabbits and donkeys and otters and hedgehogs and birds and kittens, and amongst them all was Boots, running around and having lots

of fun. She could see Rocky and Scruffy
and Mistletoe all running round as if
they were real animals, and Merry was
rubbing herself against her legs. There
were lots of people too. She could see
Rosie, and her friend Sita who lived in
Australia, and even Alfie the new boy

was there, laughing. Then there was
the sound of sleigh bells, and suddenly
Father Christmas and a sweet little
white reindeer were there too. Father
Christmas smiled at her so kindly and
Lucy felt happy from head to toe as he
held out a rolled piece of paper to her.

Everybody seemed to be such good friends, and Lucy woke up with a big smile on her face, holding out her hand to take the paper from Father Christmas. She was a bit disappointed to find her hand empty and to just be in her bedroom on her own, as normal. She looked over at Rocky. He seemed to be rocking back and forth a little, but when she blinked he was still again.

'Oh, it was just a dream,' Lucy said, disappointed, but then she looked over to the table with the snow globe. The snow was falling inside the globe, even though she hadn't shaken it since the night before, and there was something shining on the table beside it. It was a rolled up piece of paper, tied with a silver ribbon, just like the one Father Christmas had been handing to her in her dream.

'So the dream was true!' said Lucy. She felt a bit trembly as she sat up in bed and reached over for the sparkling paper beside the snow globe. She always felt that the snow globe was special, especially around Christmas, but sometimes she wondered if she was just imagining it to be magic. But Father Christmas had heard her wish on the snow globe and she was sure that the paper he had left was going to help her find a family for Boots. She just hoped that she wouldn't have to bring Boots over to the new family before she had time to spend the holiday with him.

'I mustn't be mean,' she said out

loud. 'Boots needs a family, just like Merry has ours,' and she pulled the end of the ribbon bow to undo it. The ribbon flew up into the air and disappeared in a flash. When Lucy unrolled the paper there was a sound of tinkling bells, and lots of little stars flew into the air. Merry sat up and tried to pat them, almost as if she was a kitten again. The handwritten words on the roll followed them, jumping off the paper and spelling themselves in silver, curly writing out into the air above Lucy's head.

'Hello Lucy!' Lucy could hear Father Christmas's deep, warm voice as the words formed before her. 'Friendship

is the answer!' Then, with some more sleigh bells, the words vanished into thin air, followed by the paper, and Lucy could not hear Father Christmas's voice any more.

Lucy blinked again.

'What happened there?' she said to Merry, who was chasing around the bed and lifting her paws as if she was still trying to catch the words.

'I wonder what Father Christmas meant? How can friendship be the way to find a new home for Boots?' wondered Lucy, but she felt quite pleased and relieved that it wasn't time to bring Boots to his new family just yet. 'Well, I'd love

to be a good friend to Boots,' she said.
'I'd better go over to Gran's as soon as I
can.'

Lucy had breakfast quickly then ran
upstairs and put the snow globe in her
pocket before setting off for Gran's.

'I might need you,' she thought. It
was always good to have a magic snow
globe on your side.

'I got up early and have sorted out all the animals already,' said Gran when Lucy arrived. 'Shall we take Boots for a walk? He is only just getting used to the lead, so he may get a bit excited and try to bite it, but if we can get him walking nicely that will really help when we try to re-home him.'

Boots was a bit naughty at first with the lead. Lucy managed to attach it to his collar, but first of all he lay on his back and wriggled and tried to bite it. He put his head on one side and looked at Lucy as he was doing it, and it was hard not to laugh or to tickle his sweet little furry tummy, but Lucy didn't want to reward

him for being naughty. Then he got up

but immediately sat down and refused to

move even though Lucy gently pulled on

the lead. She didn't want to pull too hard

in case it hurt his neck.

'The trick is to get him thinking that going for a walk is fun,' said Gran. 'Encourage him, make your voice sound a little higher, and he will get caught up in the excitement and want to be with you.'

'Come on Boots! Come on Boots! We're going for a WALK!' said Lucy.

It definitely worked—even a little TOO well. Boots got up, but then he started jumping up at Lucy and yelping, his tail wagging, and then he tried to pull on the lead and run ahead of Lucy as they went out the door, nearly tripping her up in his rush.

'Now stop,' said Gran. 'Don't let him go through the door in front of you. You are taking HIM for a walk, not him taking you for a walk.'

Eventually they got him out of the door and down the path, although Gran insisted that they stopped every time he pulled ahead too hard. He was panting and whimpering and wagging his tail with excitement. After not wanting to go out, he now thought walks were the best thing ever.

Gran showed Lucy how to keep Boots walking to heel by giving him little puppy treats every time he was in the right position beside her, and praising him lots. He was such a clever puppy that he improved very quickly, and Gran and Lucy beamed at each other as they walked along the road. Lucy was so used to cleaning up after animals she didn't mind using a poo bag to pick up his little poos when he stopped to do some, and when he did a long wee against a lamppost Gran said, 'Good—that's one less puddle to clear up indoors. This walk is a big success.' They went to throw the poo bag in the bin, and then Boots' ears pricked up, and he started staring at something and barking.

It was Gran's friend Comfort on her mobility scooter. Everybody loved

Comfort. She had been a midwife and district nurse in the area and seemed to be friends with everyone. Now that she found it hard to walk around, she whizzed about on her mobility scooter, chatting to people.

'Good morning, Elizabeth! Good morning, Lucy!' said Comfort, smiling broadly. 'Let me pat that sweet little puppy!'

Lucy had stepped back with Boots so he wasn't scared, and now they slowly approached. Comfort put on her warmest, most encouraging voice and leant over, calling him.

'What's his name?' she said.

'Boots,' said Lucy. 'Because he has four black legs and four little white paws, like little boots.'

Soon brave Boots was sitting on the mobility scooter step and having a fuss made of him.

'Thank you, Elizabeth. Thank you, Lucy,' said Comfort. 'That lovely little puppy has cheered me up today. I was worrying about my grandson and whether he is lonely. He and my daughter and her husband have recently moved in with me in my little flat, while they look for work and a house down here. My grandson would love a puppy but we have no room for one,' sighed Comfort. 'He loves all animals. He has gone off with his binoculars to look for birds.'

As they continued their walk, so many people stopped to say 'hello' to Gran and Lucy with Boots. Lucy had never felt so popular. They all asked the puppy's name and made a fuss of him. The postman had treats in his pocket, and gave Boots some when he sat down for him. A lady sitting on a bench, wrapped up warm and reading a book, thought he was lovely.

'Boots reminds me of my little dog, Stan,' she said. 'I miss him so much.'

A mum with small children crossed the road and came and asked if they could pat Boots, and he was very good with them.

'Having a puppy makes you lots of friends!' said Lucy to Gran.

They walked on and Boots started pulling very hard towards a boy who was standing on his own, one hand outstretched, looking up into a tree. There was a sound of fluttering wings from the tree.

'My goodness! Look at that!' said Gran. 'Look at all those birds flying down on that boy's hand. Look how they trust him. That's remarkable.'

Boots was so determined to get to get to him that he somehow managed to pull the lead out of Lucy's hand and scampered towards the boy, yelping with joy. The startled birds rose up in a tweeting, fluttering crowd and hid in the branches.

'I'm so sorry,' panted Lucy. 'Oh, hello Alfie! I didn't see it was you! That's amazing about the birds!'

Alfie was already making a fuss of Boots, who was absolutely delighted to be stroked by him. He threw himself down on his back and Alfie tickled him.

'Hello there!' he said to the puppy, but he didn't reply to Lucy, who made sure she had got a firm hold of the naughty little dog's lead this time.

'Hello,' said Gran. 'Are you Comfort's grandson, by any chance?'

Alfie nodded, blushing a little.

'I'm good friends with your grandmother. I run a wildlife rescue centre here.'

'Oh,' said Alfie, looking very interested but still not saying much.

'Your grandmother says you love animals. That was extraordinary how you got those birds to settle on your hand. Maybe you would like to come over and see my rescue centre?' said Gran.

Alfie nodded.

'If you go back to your grandmother and ask her, she will tell you where we are, and maybe you can come to lunch?' said Gran. 'Come in an hour?'

Alfie nodded again, patted Boots and set off, still without looking at Lucy.

'But Gran, what are we going to talk to him about during lunch?' said Lucy. 'All he did was nod. He was really rude too. He didn't say hello to me at all.'

'I think he's just a bit shy, Lucy. Some people are better with animals than people. I'm sure Boots will help him come out of his shell,' said Gran.

'I hope so,' Lucy said.

Chapter Three

By the time they got back to Gran's, Boots was very tired. Gran had made a lovely little cosy den for him in his dog crate. He had his blankets and a cuddly teddy, and Lucy hid some tiny treats in the folds of his blanket for him to find when he woke up.

'This way he sees being in his crate as a happy, secure thing,' said Gran, gently closing the door on the sleepy puppy. 'Now, he is safe inside and hopefully we can get on with sorting out lunch and doing some jobs.'

They went into the wildlife centre attached to Gran's house, leaving the door to the kitchen open so they could hear Boots when he woke up. Lucy swept and mopped the floor. Then she helped Gran clean out some cages, making

48

sure to be very quiet and calm around the animals. At Christmas time there were always lots of small hedgehogs who were too small to survive hibernating during the winter. People brought them to Gran and she got rid of any ticks they had, and wormed them, fed them dog food and weighed them every day to check they were growing bigger. Although it was hard work cleaning the floor and cages and then washing out bowls and syringes and equipment, Lucy always felt very glad to be helping Gran. She knew how important it was to make sure the animals were happy and cosy and safe. She was sure the squirrel with the cut on his tummy would get well quicker with fresh bedding, even though he chattered crossly at them as they swept out the cage.

'We really need to dress that rabbit's paw again after lunch,' said Gran. 'Poor thing, it is still very nervous. And that squirrel isn't looking very pleased with me, but Nieve the vet said it needs antibiotics after being bitten by a dog so I must give them.'

'It's a shame they don't know we're their friends and we are helping them,' said Lucy.

'The important thing is that we are, though,' said Gran. 'They can't help being cross with us, or shy. They are wild animals, not pets like little Boots. Let's wash our hands and sort out lunch before Alfie comes and Boots wakes up.'

There was a knock at the door and Alfie arrived.

'Welcome to my little rescue centre,' said Gran, smiling, bringing him in.

Alfie looked very interested to see all the cages.

'I used to help out at a rescue centre and city farm in London,' he said. 'They had small wild animals and also donkeys and sheep and goats.'

Lucy had never heard Alfie say so much.

'Well, we have to dress that rabbit's paw. Would you like to get him out for me?' said Gran.

Alfie nodded. He stood in front of the rabbit's cage and opened the door. Then he went very still for a moment, reached in, and then suddenly the rabbit was held securely in his arms, not struggling at all.

'That was wonderful!' exclaimed Gran, as she examined the rabbit's paw. 'You were so calm, yet quick, and he didn't have time to get stressed.'

Boots had obviously woken up in

the kitchen. They could hear him whining and scratching at his crate door.

'Lucy—could you scoop Boots up and put him out in the garden?' said Gran, finishing off dressing the rabbit's foot. 'Then make sure he doesn't rush in when we are dealing with the squirrel. Are you confident with squirrels too, Alfie? I will give you some thick gloves as he really is very cross.'

Lucy took Boots out into the garden for his wee, then picked him up and walked carefully into the room. She was very experienced at helping Gran now, and she knew how difficult handling the squirrel would be, but also how important it was that he got his medicine. When she got back into the room the squirrel was still in his cage.

'Shall I put Boots back in the crate while you do the squirrel?' said Lucy.

'We've done him!' beamed Gran. 'I think we will have to call Alfie a squirrel-whisperer. I've never seen anything like it.'

Alfie was standing next to the cage quietly talking to the squirrel, who seemed to be listening to him.

Gran had already made some lovely carrot soup and homemade bread, and it was a very happy lunch. Alfie was a shy person, but he loved animals so much that he asked Gran and Lucy lots of questions about the centre, and he listened very well. Lucy loved telling him about the otter and the rabbit and the hedgehogs, and all the animals on her badges.

'I like the donkey badge!' he said, his brown eyes looking sad. 'I miss the donkey at the city farm.'

'Why don't you take Alfie to Rosie's farm after lunch and he can meet Pixie and Elf and the others?' said Gran. 'You could take Boots with you—he needs exercise.'

Boots was sitting on Alfie's foot, pulling at his laces. They tried to keep him entertained during lunch, rolling balls for him across the room as they ate their soup, but he kept coming back and trying to get their attention, especially Alfie's.

'Would you like a dog?' said Lucy.

Alfie fondled Boot's ears. 'I'd love one, but we don't have a house at the moment. Dad was ill and Mum lost her job, so Gran invited us to come and live with her here.'

'I'm sorry,' said Lucy.

'I do like being in the country,' said Alfie. 'But I miss my friends and the city farm. It's nice being here today. Thank you for the lunch. Would you like help washing up?'

'That's all right, Alfie,' said Gran, smiling at him. 'Tell you what. I'll wash up if you and Lucy take Boots out,' said Gran. 'Lucy—take some money and you and Alfie can have a hot chocolate at the café when you are out. I think that if you are missing the city farm, Alfie, you'll love Rosie's farm.'

Lucy put Boots on the lead and they walked to the farm again. They passed the lady sitting on the bench with her book who they had seen the day before.

'Oh, hello Boots!' she said, delightedly.

Boots was very pleased to have a fuss made of him.

'I do miss having a dog. It's lonely where I live now my husband has died. I put on my coat and fingerless gloves and come and sit here and read and talk to passersby to cheer myself up.

You probably think I'm a silly old lady

doing that,' she said, making a face and

laughing a little as if it was a joke, but

Lucy felt sad. It must be hard not to have

friends. She would miss Rosie so much

if she wasn't there, and even though Sita was in Australia, she and Rosie Skyped her and emailed her and sent each other cards. And now there was Alfie—Lucy had a feeling he was going to be a friend too.

'Well, it's lovely meeting you both and Boots,' said the lady, being very cheerful again. 'My name is Jennifer, by the way. What are your names?'

'Alfie and Lucy,' said Lucy, suddenly having a brilliant idea. 'Could you have a puppy? My Gran is trying to find a good home for Boots.'

'I'd love one, dear, but I know dogs. Boots will need lots of walks and I'm not really up to that,' said the lady, sadly. Then she put a brave smile on again. 'But thank you all the same.'

They said goodbye to Jennifer and walked on. Alfie took Boots' lead. It was cold, and Lucy had forgotten her gloves, so she put her hands in her pockets and thought about how Jennifer must be cold sitting on the bench like that.

Lucy felt the cold glass of the snow globe.

'I wish Jennifer had some friends and somewhere warm to go. I think I'll tell Gran about her,' said Lucy out loud. And then she felt the globe get warm under her fingers. She really wanted to take it out and see what was happening, but Alfie was there and she didn't know how to explain it.

Thank you for warming my hands, thought Lucy. *I wonder if you are also going to grant my wish for Jennifer. I hope so.* She felt happy at the thought.

Lucy and Alfie and Boots walked down the long lane to Rosie's farm, past winter hedges and spiky bare trees. A robin followed them, singing.

'I know that robins sing to warn others away from their territory,' said Lucy, 'but I can't help thinking they are friendly birds.' As if to prove her words, the robin suddenly flew down onto Alfie's

shoulder before flying off again, singing.

Boots was very startled and outraged that the robin had sat on Alfie's shoulder, and made a big fuss, yelping and barking and trying to run after the robin.

'Calm down, Boots,' said Alfie, who had the lead. Boots reluctantly gave up, obviously realizing that he couldn't fly, and came and sat at Alfie's feet.

'What happened there?' said Lucy.

'I suppose I just like birds!' said Alfie, a bit shyly.

'I like birds too,' said Lucy, 'but they don't come and fly to my hands and on my shoulders like they do to you!'

'I did have some food in my hands

the other day,' said Alfie.

'Yes, but that's still incredible. And you don't have any food on your shoulder!' laughed Lucy. It would be easy to feel jealous of Alfie, but he was so kind and gentle that Lucy just felt really amazed and glad to have met him. She had never had a friend like him!

Boots is making so many friends. Maybe that's what Father Christmas meant when he said that friendship would help him, thought Lucy, watching Alfie pet Boots. *But I still don't understand how that works because even though we are all Boots' friends now, none of us can help him*

*with what he needs most of all. Gran
and I can't have him. Neither can Alfie
or Jennifer, and Gran says that Rosie's
family can't take him either. Boots has
lots of friends . . . what he needs is a
home. How are we going to find him
one?* She touched the globe again—it
was still warm.

*I don't know how you are going to
do this, but I know you can help,* said
Lucy in her head to the snow globe as
she held it, round and mysteriously
warm and comforting in her pocket.
*Please find Boots a special home for
Christmas.*

Chapter Four

'Hello Lucy! Hello Alfie!' said Rosie, coming to meet them. 'Is this your puppy, Alfie?'

Boots barked and wagged his tail as if to say 'Yes', but Alfie shook his head.

'Alfie and his parents are living with his gran, so there isn't room,' said Lucy. 'Gran is looking after him.'

'Oh, you're Boots!' said Rosie, squatting down to make a proper fuss of the happy little dog. 'Your gran asked Mum and Dad if we could have him. I wish we could. It's just that everybody is so busy—there is so much work to do fixing fences and working on the farm, and in the café, and then we've got a new rescue donkey and she is really scared. Even Nieve the vet couldn't touch her yesterday—she is going to come this morning to try again.'

'Can we show Pixie and Elf to Alfie?' asked Lucy. 'Pixie and Elf are the first donkeys Rosie's family had,' she explained to Alfie. 'We saw Elf just after he was born. Our friend Sita named him before she went back to Australia, and we show him to her by Skype.'

They made their way to the stables and the fields where the donkeys were. Pixie and Elf immediately rushed over, and Boots hid behind Alfie's legs for a bit, but Alfie ignored him and Boots was too curious to stay hiding for long. He approached the fence slowly, and Pixie put her head down to look at him. Boots looked up at her and wagged his tail.

'Boots is making friends!' said Rosie. Little Elf trotted over too, but as he came nearer he reversed so that he could have his bottom scratched. 'He wants a scratch!' laughed Alfie. 'What a clever little donkey!'

Then Teddy and Snowy, two very friendly old rescue donkeys trotted over too.

'Hello,' said Alfie, a big smile on his face, as he scratched their backs.

'I was going to tell you that donkeys liked being scratched rather than patted,' said Rosie, 'but I can see you know that already.'

'I love donkeys,' said Alfie. 'I used to work with them at the city farm.'

Boots was a bit jealous of all the fuss the donkeys were having. He barked and jumped up at Alfie for attention.

'Look—there's Nieve. She came to check on our new donkey, Tess,' said Rosie. 'She doesn't look happy. Let's go and see.'

Nieve was standing by the stables talking to Rosie's mum and dad, and even at a distance you could see from the way that she was standing and waving her arms that she wasn't happy.

As they got nearer they could hear her saying, 'That donkey is so scared of people I don't want to stress her out even more. I'm really worried that she seems so sad and won't come out or eat. I really do need to know if she is in pain. If she would only let me look in her mouth.'

They looked over a half stable door and saw a small donkey in the corner of the stable.

'Come and have a cup of tea,' said Rosie's mum. 'Hello Lucy! And who is this?'

'Alfie,' said Alfie, a little shyly.

'And who is this?' said Nieve, bending down to pet Boots, who rushed over to be made a fuss of.

Maybe Nieve will be able to adopt

Boots! thought Lucy, happily.

But as she tickled him Nieve said, 'Your Gran asked me if I would like to adopt him, but I don't think my two old dogs would cope with a boisterous puppy, and I'm so busy at the clinic and on visits I couldn't really take him with me. It's such a shame, as he is a great little dog.'

Oh no, thought Lucy. *Another friend for Boots but still no new home.*

'Nieve!' said Rosie's mum quietly to her. 'Just look over there!'

Lucy turned to see what they were looking at. Alfie was standing at the half stable door quietly talking to the little donkey who had come right up to him. He was gently scratching her neck and she seemed to be listening to him.

'I can hardly believe it!' said Nieve to Rosie's mum.

'That's amazing!' whispered Rosie to Lucy. Nobody wanted to disturb Alfie and the donkey.

'You should have seen him at the rescue centre,' said Lucy. 'Gran called him a squirrel-whisperer!'

'Well, he's obviously a donkey-whisperer too,' said Nieve. She stood up and went to walk slowly over to Alfie, but Boots ruined things by jumping up excitedly and barking and running after her and then to Alfie. The donkey started and ran back to the corner of the stable, where she stood, her head down.

'How did you do that?' said Nieve to Alfie, as Lucy ran after Boots and got hold of his lead. He wasn't pleased and kept trying to get to Alfie.

Alfie shrugged, blushing a little.

'Well, I'd love it if you could help me with this donkey,' said Nieve. 'Do you think you could do that?'

Alfie nodded. 'Yes, I'd like to.'

'We'd need to get permission from your parents though,' said Nieve. 'Scared donkeys can kick out, as I am sure you know, and like all animals they can nip, although I have a feeling that she wouldn't with you.'

'I'd definitely rather talk to your mum and dad first,' said Rosie's mum. 'I want to help poor Tess. She was found neglected, alone in a field, and I want her to have a happy life here, but I don't want you hurt, as donkeys are strong. Do you think I could phone your mum and dad tonight and ask?'

'Um, yes,' said Alfie, shyly, and wrote down his mum and dad's telephone numbers for her.

'That would be wonderful,' said Nieve. 'I'd like to come tomorrow afternoon and try again. Would you be able to be here then, Alfie?'

Alfie nodded, looking very happy, as he stroked Boots. Lucy felt glad. Alfie had only been at their school for a couple of weeks, but he hadn't seemed very confident there. Here, he looked at home and not worried at all.

'Come and have some tea and cake!' said Rosie's mum. She led the way into the new café they had opened. There was a glass counter with a cake stand with lots of lovely cakes, and some tables with checked tablecloths and painted wooden chairs. It looked clean and welcoming, but there were no customers.

'We really need to advertise more,' said Rosie's mum. 'But we have been so busy with the farm and the donkeys and getting the kitchen ready so that we can sell food, that we haven't done that.

I don't think many people know we are here.'

'I could help make posters,' said Lucy.

'We could ask if we could put them in the shop windows in town,' said Rosie. 'Everyone is doing their Christmas shopping so they will see them.'

'I'll put one up in the vet's and tell everyone on the newsletter,' said Nieve.

'Would you like to stay here and make some posters with us?' said Rosie to Alfie.

'Yes, please,' said Alfie, and smiled at her and Lucy.

'Maybe we could Skype Sita later this week,' said Lucy to Rosie. 'She should have got our presents and cards by now. We could show her Boots. Sita is our friend who went back to live in Australia,' she explained to Alfie. 'She likes animals too.'

'Have some lemon drizzle cake,' said Rosie's mum.

While Nieve and Rosie's mum chatted, Rosie, Alfie, and Lucy took Boots and sat at a table to make posters. Rosie went and got some pens and card.

After his walk and all the excitement, Boots fell fast asleep at Lucy's feet while they ate the yummy lemon drizzle cake

Rosie's mum had made. Then Leah, Rosie's little sister, came back from shopping with her dad and helped make more posters for the café.

'We can ask if we can put one up in the village hall,' said Rosie, holding up a finished poster to admire. 'Leah's dance class is there tomorrow—I am going to take her there.'

'I'll take Boots and walk down there and meet you and Leah tomorrow morning, Rosie,' said Lucy.

'You can come back to ours for lunch tomorrow,' said Rosie. 'Bring Boots! It will be good for him to get used to donkeys.'

'Alfie can come too!' said Leah, who really liked this new boy.

'Of course,' said Rosie. 'Alfie, do you want to meet us at the village hall?'

'OK,' said Alfie.

'I think we'd better go now,' said

Lucy. 'It's getting dark and Gran will be at my house. She is making dinner again and Oscar is coming back from his school trip. We are going to watch a Christmas film. I love the holidays!'

They woke Boots. Alfie waved goodbye as Lucy went to walk Boots back up the lane.

'I think I'll just stay here a little bit more with Tess and get her used to me,' he said. 'I want her to feel safe and calm when she sees Nieve the vet tomorrow.'

Alfie patted Boots, who whined and tried to climb up Alfie's legs.

'No, Boots. I will see you tomorrow,' said Alfie. 'Be a good boy and go with

Lucy.' That seemed to settle the puppy. Boots did keep hopefully turning and looking back until they had left the farm behind and Alfie disappeared from view, and then he trotted along beside Lucy.

'I'm sorry, Boots. I think you should live with Alfie too. I wish we could find a way for that to happen,' said Lucy, and went to get a dog treat to give to the fluffy little puppy walking so well beside her. As she put her hand in her coat pocket she felt the snow globe warm again, and at the same time, something cold and wet landed on her nose.

'It's snowing!' she said, looking up into the sky as snow fell quickly all around them. Boots was very excited by all the flakes whirling about. Lucy suddenly felt very Christmassy and very happy.

'Come on Boots—I think tomorrow is going to be even better than today!' she laughed.

Chapter Five

Gran made a warm stew, and apple
crumble and custard, while Lucy played
with Boots and fed him. She went out
into the dark night garden with him.

He got very excited, running around and barking at the snowflakes falling in the light from the kitchen. It was quite hard to get him to come back inside!

'He's gorgeous!' said Oscar, arriving back with Mum and Dad. Lucy was glad to see him. Oscar could be an annoying big brother sometimes, but he was fun and kind too. Boots was extremely pleased to meet a new, big boy, and happily spent the rest of the night cuddled up on Oscar's or Lucy's laps as they all watched a Christmas film together. Then Gran took Boots home. The snow had stopped for the moment, but it had settled enough for Boots to make sweet little paw prints in the snow as they left.

'I'll come and help you tomorrow morning,' said Lucy, kissing Gran goodnight.

'Thank you, Lucy,' said Gran. 'I'm so lucky to have such a kind granddaughter.'

'I'll come and help you too this holiday,' said Oscar, giving Gran a hug. 'I'm going to have a lie-in tomorrow, but I said I'd help Dad get the Christmas tree at the farm tomorrow afternoon—shall I get yours too and help put it up at the centre?'

'That would be lovely, Oscar. What a lucky Gran I am!' said Gran smiling, and waved them goodbye.

Lucy took the snow globe out of

her pocket and put it back next to her bed. She shook it and the snow whirled around the way it had started whirling around again outside.

'I wish we could find a home for Boots,' Lucy whispered, but it didn't change. It just looked like a normal, pretty snow globe, with snow falling over a little forest and a cottage. 'I'm sure I felt you grow warm in my pocket today,' she said. 'I'm not exactly sure what is going on, but you've never let me down before.'

Merry came in. She was shaking her paws one by one, daintily.

'Have you been out in the snow?' said

Lucy. 'I can see you didn't enjoy it like Boots!' Merry took a leap up onto the bed and butted her head against Lucy's, purring loudly. She was a little cold and damp, but Lucy didn't mind.

'Oh, I do love you, Merry,' said Lucy, and as the snow fell in the snow globe and outside in the garden and her cat curled up beside her on top of the duvet, Lucy closed her eyes and fell asleep.

The next morning Oscar was still asleep when Lucy got up and went to Gran's. Just before she left, she ran back upstairs

and put the snow globe in her pocket.
She wasn't exactly sure why.

'Perhaps you will help me find a new
home for Boots, today,' she said.

The snow had stopped but was much
deeper after falling overnight, and had
covered up Boots' paw prints. The sky
was grey and it was cold. It looked like it
might snow again.

Lucy helped Gran and then took
Boots for a walk on her own around the
village.

'Keep a firm hold on his lead, Lucy,'
said Gran. 'He is such a wiggly little
puppy—we don't want him running off.'

Boots was so happy—his little tail was

wagging and Lucy had to keep stopping to teach him not to pull so hard.

'Slow down, Boots!' she laughed. 'It can't be comfortable pulling like that!'

Lucy noticed Jennifer, well wrapped up, standing by the village green feeding the birds.

'Hello Lucy! Hello Boots!' said Jennifer, patting him. 'I thought I'd come out and make sure the village birds had enough to eat.'

The mum they had seen before was walking to the village hall with her baby in her pram.

'Hello Boots!' she said. 'My little girl Tabitha will be pleased to see you again.

I'm collecting her from dancing.'

Lucy arrived at the village hall with Boots just as all the children were coming out from their class. Rosie came out with Leah and Leah's friends—one of them was Tabitha. They all rushed over to Boots to make a fuss of him, while Lucy talked to Rosie.

'People were very interested in our poster,' said Rosie, happily. 'They said they would like somewhere to have tea in the village, and they didn't know there was a new tea room at the farm.'

Boots was having a lovely time being fussed by so many children, when suddenly a very loud car alarm went off.

Lucy jumped, and felt a tug on the lead, and then when she looked down she saw a lead with a collar attached, and Boots running off down the road, as fast as his little legs could take him.

'Oh no! Boots! Come back!' called Lucy, running after him, but it was surprising how fast a puppy could run, and he wasn't listening.

'I'll get him!' came Comfort's voice. She had driven up in her motor scooter, and was with a man and a woman and Alfie.

'What's happened?' said Alfie to Lucy, as his grandmother drove off along the snowy path after Boots.

'Be careful, Mum,' said Alfie's mum, and she and Alfie's dad ran after her.

'I'm so sorry,' said Tabitha's mum to Lucy, pushing the pram. 'I feel responsible. I should have noticed the puppy's collar had got loose when the children were stroking him. We'll come and help.'

Some other adults and children said they would come too. Everyone was very upset that Boots had run off and everyone followed Comfort.

They passed Jennifer. 'What's going on?' she said, as children and adults passed her. 'I thought I saw Boots run past, but he was too fast to stop. Has he run off? I think he went down there.'

'Oh good, that's the way to the farm,' said Rosie, and the line of people turned down the path.

'I can see his paw prints!' called Comfort.

Everyone was cheered up by that, and it was true that the puppy's prints were clear to see.

'We'll soon find him!' called Comfort, but then, all of a sudden, it started snowing so heavily that within minutes they could hardly see. They had reached the end of the path and the farm café was lit up, so everyone headed for it. Rosie's mum opened the door and looked very startled as a crowd of people rushed inside.

'What's happening?' she said.

Lucy burst into tears.

'Boots has slipped his lead,' said Rosie, putting her arm around Lucy's shoulders. 'We saw him run down here, but then it started snowing and we couldn't see anything.'

'He's so small, and he is lost in a blizzard,' Lucy cried.

'We'll find him,' said Alfie. 'Don't

cry, Lucy. I'm sure Boots is about.'

'Hello—what's going on?' came a familiar voice. 'What's the matter, Lucy?' It was Dad with Oscar and Mum and Gran. Oscar and Dad were carrying Christmas trees they had just bought from Peter, Rosie's stepdad. Mum and Gran rushed over to give Lucy a hug while Rosie told them what had happened.

'I'm so sorry, Gran,' sniffed Lucy. 'It's all my fault.'

'Don't worry, Lucy. I'm sure we can find him soon. Maybe it would be better if there weren't crowds out looking—lots of excited children might scare him a bit,' said Gran. 'Why don't some of us stay here and keep the children occupied, and some go out and search the farm?'

Rosie's mum explained the plan to everyone: the younger children and their mums would stay warm in the café while Oscar, Mum, Dad, Peter, Alfie and his parents, Lucy, and Rosie would look around the farm for Boots.

The mums and children settled in at tables, glad to be out of the cold, and exclaimed how pretty everything was.

'The only problem is, what am I going to do with all these customers?' said Rosie's mum worriedly to Lucy's mum. 'If they all want hot drinks and cakes I will be rushed off my feet.'

'I'll help!' said Jennifer, who had taken off her coat and scarf. 'I used to work in a café. I'd love to make teas.'

'And I can help too,' said Alfie's mum.

'You can look out the window and see if you can spot Boots. That would be a GREAT help,' said Rosie's mum, when the littlest children wanted to join in the search. 'We don't want you getting lost as well. And Leah will get you some paper and crayons, and you can draw some lovely pictures for me to put up around the café.'

Gran and Lucy's mum stayed with the children and pointed out things they could see through the window—it helped that a little robin came and hopped around just by the glass, and didn't seem scared at all by all the people looking at him, and then some rabbits appeared out of nowhere, playing in the snow. Lucy's mum helped other children draw pictures. Alfie's mum and Rosie's mum went behind the counter while Jennifer went around the tables and took orders.

The search party set out.

'Oh no! The new snow has covered up all the paw prints,' said Lucy.

'I wish the fences didn't have so many

holes in them,' said Peter, worriedly. 'I've been trying to fix up the farm, but it's hard doing it all on my own, and I'm not that experienced.'

'I could help you, if you like,' said Alfie's dad. 'I'm good at fixing things.'

'That would be great!' said Peter. 'I need someone to work with me to do up the farm, so I could pay you. We need someone to fix things and make sure the paths can be used by people with prams and wheelchairs and mobility scooters.'

'I can definitely do that!' said Alfie's dad, smiling. 'And I've been looking for a job, so this is perfect!'

Lucy would have been happy to

hear this, but she was too worried about Boots. Suddenly she remembered the snow globe. She put her hand in her pocket and felt the cold surface of the little globe. She was so glad she had put it in her pocket that morning. Her heart started beating faster. She let the adults and Oscar go on ahead, as they split off in different directions calling 'Boots! Boots!'

She waited with Rosie and Alfie and took the globe out. There wasn't time to feel shy. Little Boots was lost and they had to find him.

'Why have you got your snow globe with you?' said Rosie, puzzled.

'I don't know why. I put it in my pocket as I was going out this morning, and I think I am meant to wish on it now,' said Lucy, and before Alfie and Rosie could ask any more questions, she put her hands round the globe and wished: 'Please show us where Boots is.'

Suddenly the globe glowed warmly, and the snow started falling inside. But then it turned from white sparkling flakes to rainbow-coloured ones. For a moment, a picture of a donkey appeared in the globe, and then Alfie and Rosie and Lucy all seemed to be standing in a cloud of rainbow-coloured dancing flakes. It was over in a minute.

'What was that?' said Alfie, laughing in amazement.

'I don't know,' said Rosie, blinking.

Lucy was looking into the snow globe. It was just the same as normal again, but now she knew where Boots was.

'Come on!' Lucy said, putting the globe back in her pocket, and led the way to Tess's stable.

And there Boots was. The little black-and-white puppy was curled up with Tess, who was nuzzling him. And they looked like the best of friends.

Chapter Six

'I think Boots was looking for you, Alfie,'
said Lucy. 'Do you remember how jealous
he was when he saw you with Tess? The
last time he saw you was at the stable.

I think he got scared and came here to find you, and managed to crawl through that hole at the bottom of the stable door and get in with Tess.'

'We're very lucky Tess didn't kick him,' said Nieve's voice behind them. 'She seems to have completely accepted him. Hello everyone! I heard from the café that you were out looking for Boots. I'm glad you found him!'

'So am I!' said Lucy, suddenly feeling wobbly with relief.

Alfie had let himself into the stable, and was kneeling down, talking gently to Tess while Alfie, wagging his tail and wiggling and whimpering in delight, jumped up and pawed at Alfie until he gave in and picked the excited puppy up in his arms. Boots licked his nose and barked. Tess didn't seem scared at all. She just looked trustfully at Alfie with her beautiful big eyes.

'Oh Boots,' said Alfie, cuddling the puppy. Lucy could hear in his voice how much he loved the little puppy. 'I wish I had a home so that I could adopt you.'

Suddenly Lucy heard the sound of sleigh bells. Rosie must have heard them too as she frowned and looked over at her.

'Did you hear that?' Rosie mouthed.

Lucy put her hand in her pocket.

The snow globe was still there, and it was glowing warm again. Something wonderful was going to happen. Lucy was sure of it.

Alfie's dad's voice broke in. He and the others had seen the group gathered by the stable and had come to investigate.

'Alfie—if that's what you want, you can have him! Peter's just offered me a job on the farm, and there's a house which goes with it. Boots can come and live with us.'

Lucy had never seen a wider smile on anyone's face until she looked over at Alfie. He wiped his eyes with his sleeve and gave Boots a tight cuddle.

'You're mine, Boots!' he said. 'I can't believe it! My own dog at last, and the best dog I could ever have imagined.' Boots gave a contented little woof as if he agreed, and everybody laughed.

'Now Boots, you've got to be a good boy and go with Lucy so that I can help Tess and Nieve,' said Alfie. 'Go to the café with them and I will join you.' He handed Lucy the puppy, who seemed to understand what was happening and settled happily into Lucy's arms, yawning after all the excitement. He had got his boy at last, and now he could relax.

They all went to the café, and

everyone was so happy to see Boots was safe and well.

'We've had such a good day!' said Rosie's mum to Peter and Rosie. 'Everybody loves the café. It's been so busy! The mums want to have a mother and toddler group here twice a week, and Comfort is going to run a computer club for the old-age pensioners. She has suggested that your grandad and the other people in his home all come here to join in too.'

'Will you be able to cope with a busy café as well as organizing the conservation centre?' said Peter, looking concerned.

'Yes, now that Alfie's mum, Grace, and Jennifer are here. I've offered them part-time jobs, and they've said yes!'

Jennifer and Grace both looked very busy and happy.

'Well, Dan here, Alfie's dad, is going to be the handyman we have been needing,' said Peter. 'He is going to do up the cottages—one for his family, and one he said could be a holiday cottage!'

Everybody beamed at each other.

Lucy felt in her pocket. 'Thank you, magic snow globe,' she whispered.

'Well, that was such a great story!' said Sita. She was on Skype with Lucy and Rosie. They were in Lucy's bedroom, and she had borrowed the laptop. It was Christmas Eve, and Lucy and Rosie had wanted to wish their Australian friend happy Christmas and tell her all about their new friend Alfie. 'I really want to meet Alfie and Boots now, and I'm so glad Tess the donkey is so happy and is friends with all the other donkeys too. I've got exciting news as well. Dad says we can come back on holiday to England next year, so I will see you all!'

'Maybe you can stay in our new holiday cottage on the farm. Alfie's dad will have it done by then!' said Rosie.

'I can't wait!' said Sita, happily.

'Neither can we,' said Lucy and Rosie together, and laughed.

'Happy Christmas!' said Lucy. 'I can't believe you are going to have a barbecue on the beach when we are going to be sledging in the snow! But I'm sure whatever we do, it'll be fun!'

'Happy Christmas!' said Sita back. 'See you again soon!'

Thank you . . .

To Anne Clark, my lovely agent, and to
Clare Whitston, Deborah Sims and Liz Cross
and all at OUP for their work on the Lucy
books. Especial thanks to the amazing
illustrator Sophy Williams and designers
Sarah Darby and Justin Hoffmann for
making this book so beautiful.

I have met two wonderful nurses called
Comfort, so I named Alfie's grandmother
after them. I also was inspired by my
friend Peggy Pryer, a retired nurse who
has a mobility scooter and is so kind to
everyone in our village!

Lastly, I would like to thank my husband
Graeme and my children, Joanna, Michael,
Laura and Christina, and our dogs Timmy
and Ben, who were both adorable puppies,
and as naughty as Boots!

About the author

Every Christmas, Anne used to ask for a dog. She had to wait many years, but now she has two dogs, called Timmy and Ben. Timmy is a big, gentle golden retriever who loves people and food and is scared of cats. Ben is a small brown and white cavalier King Charles spaniel who is a bit like a cat because he curls up in the warmest places and bosses Timmy about. He snuffles and snorts quite a lot and you can tell what he is feeling by the way he walks. He has a particularly pleased patter when he has stolen something he shouldn't have, which gives him away immediately. Anne lives in a village in Kent and is not afraid of spiders.

How to make Rosie's mum's delicious lemon drizzle cake!

Ingredients:

225g butter
225g caster sugar
4 eggs
225g self-raising flour
Finely grated zest 1 lemon

For the drizzle topping:

Juice of 1$\frac{1}{2}$ lemons
85g caster sugar

Method:

1. Heat oven to 180C/fan 160C/gas 4.

2. Beat together the butter and sugar until pale and creamy, then add the eggs one at a time, slowly mixing through.

3. Sift in flour, then add the lemon zest and stir well.

4. Line a loaf tin (8 x 21cm) with greaseproof paper, then pour in the mixture.

5. Bake for 45-50 mins until a thin skewer inserted into the centre of the cake comes out clean.

6. While the cake is cooling in its tin, mix together the lemon juice and sugar to make the drizzle.

7. Prick the warm cake all over with a skewer or fork, then pour over the drizzle – the juice will sink in and the sugar will form a lovely, crisp topping.

8. Once it's cool, enjoy!

If you enjoyed

Lucy Makes A Wish

then read on for a taster

of another of Lucy's festive

adventures,

Lucy's Search for Little Star

ANNE BOOTH

Making a wish for a Christmas miracle.

Lucy's Search for Little Star

Illustrated by Sophy Williams

Chapter One

The car headlights lit up the stone cottage at the end of the lane. The wooden door had a Christmas wreath hanging on it, and fairy lights in the windows were flashing on and off.

'Welcome to our Christmas cottage!' said Mum, stopping the car, and turning round to smile at Lucy, Gran, and Lucy's big brother, Oscar.

'Someone's been busy decorating already!' laughed Dad.

Lucy felt fizzy with excitement. After a long drive she was going to see her friend Sita again. Sita had gone back to live in Australia with her family at the beginning of the year, but she and her mum and dad had come back to England for Christmas to visit Sita's grandad, and they had rented a big holiday cottage next to a farm by the sea and had invited Lucy and her family to join them.

The front door opened and out of the brightness rushed Sita and her parents. There was lots of laughter and excitement as everyone got out of the car.

'Hello!' said Sita, a little shyly. She and Lucy had sent each other cards, and emailed and talked on Skype since she had moved back to Australia, but it felt different really being back together again.

'Hello Sita! How wonderful to see you!' said Gran, giving her a big hug, and putting her arm out to Lucy to pull her in, too. Gran made them all jump up and down, the girls laughed together, and suddenly it felt as though they had never been apart.

'I'm so glad you could all come,' said Prajit, as he carried some of their luggage and led them into the warm house.

Soon they were sitting round a big kitchen table, holding mugs of hot chocolate.

'We asked the farmer if we could decorate the house as we are staying here over Christmas, and he said "yes",' said Sita. 'We thought we could make some decorations tomorrow and buy a little Christmas tree in the town, if you like?'

'That sounds good,' said Lucy.

'You were so kind to us the first Christmas we arrived,' said Prajit. 'We wanted to treat you all.'

Sita and Lucy smiled at each other, remembering the little rabbit they had rescued and returned to his family that Christmas.

'It certainly is a treat not to have to do all the cooking for Christmas,' said Mum, 'but we can't let you do it all on your own!'

'Oscar has made a Christmas cake for us all,' said Dad.

'Good on ya, Oscar!' said Prajit.

'And Lucy and I made a Christmas pudding,' said Gran. 'We made a few, actually, to raise money for the Wildlife Rescue Centre.'

'Who will be looking after the Centre

when you are here?' Joanna asked.

'Well, that's the amazing thing,' said Gran. 'It was perfect timing! My friend Miriam, who is a retired vet, needed a holiday. She is going to stay over at my house and look after the animals, and her daughter and grandchildren are going to stay at Lucy and Oscar's and look after Merry!'

'Sorry you had to leave Merry,' said Sita to Lucy, quietly. She knew how much Lucy loved her little cat.

'It's all right,' said Lucy. 'I will miss her but I know Merry doesn't like to go away—she prefers to stay at home. And I know Miriam will make a big fuss of her.'

'I miss Twinkle too, but I know my uncle will make a big fuss of her as well,' said Sita. 'He took a picture of her yesterday and sent it to me—look.' She took out her phone and showed Lucy a sweet picture of a little black and white dog digging on a golden beach.

'When Oscar was little he tried to dig down to Australia,' said Dad. 'He thought if it was on the other side of the world he would pop up on an Australian beach.'

'Dad!' said Oscar, bringing in the cake tin from the car. 'You are so embarrassing!'

Sita's mum looked over her shoulder at the photo on the phone. 'They are going to have a barbecue on the beach for Christmas but we had to buy scarves and hats and gloves to come here!'

'Well, we won't have a barbecue, but we can definitely walk by the sea,' said Prajit.

'There is a nature reserve here too, so all you animal and bird lovers will be happy! There are even some bird hides on the dunes we can visit.'

'And look what else is here,' said Gran, pointing over at the window. 'A telescope!'

'If the skies are clear we can look at the stars,' Oscar said.

Oscar's school had a Star Centre with

a big telescope and Oscar and his friends loved it. Lucy had overheard Mum and Dad worrying that Oscar wouldn't have any friends with him over Christmas, but at least he could look at the stars. Lucy was glad she had Sita—it was so lovely to see her again.

They went upstairs to find their rooms. Sita and Lucy were sharing one at the top of the house. It was beautiful— it even had its own bathroom and a big window with a window seat. There were twin beds, each with soft white fluffy towels on them, folded and left for them to use. It was dark outside—Lucy and Sita looked at their reflections in the window and laughed and waved.

'In the morning we'll be able to see the sea from our room,' said Sita excitedly. 'You've brought Scruffy and Mistletoe!' she laughed, as she watched Lucy unpack her bag.

Lucy put Scruffy, her dog pyjama

case, and Mistletoe, her toy donkey, on the bed and finished unpacking by placing her special snow globe light on her bedside table. There was a special magic about it at this time of year, and in the past it had helped Lucy's Christmas wishes come true. She couldn't tell when it would start to glow and do its magic though, or even if there was any magic left. Most of the time it stayed a pretty snow globe, with a little cottage in a wood. It snowed when Lucy shook it, and it had a soft light in the night which Lucy loved.

'I wonder if you will grant me a special Christmas wish again this year?' thought Lucy. She touched the cool glass globe and remembered all the magic of past Christmases. The snow globe stayed the same, but Lucy still felt hopeful. The holiday had only just begun, after all.

'I love it that you brought your snow globe!' laughed Sita, and picked it up to shake it. 'I love seeing the snow fall. I wish it would snow this Christmas!'

Lucy was sure that she saw the snow globe glow brightly for a minute as the snow fell faster and faster, although Sita didn't seem to notice. Lucy felt a little bubble of excitement rise inside.

Lucy and Sita brushed their teeth and got into bed. They had so much to talk about! Lucy told Sita all about how busy their friend Rosie's farm and café was, and how Pixie the donkey and Elf, her foal, were doing. Sita showed Lucy pictures of her friends in Australia and some of the wildlife she had seen since moving.

'I love it there, but I do miss you and Rosie. And I'm looking forward to seeing Grandad tomorrow,' said Sita. 'He is bringing Charlie, his spaniel, with him! And Oscar will love talking to my grandad because he knows so much about the stars.'

Sita gave a big yawn and snuggled down under the covers.

Lucy leant over and shook the globe so that the snow fell over the little house in the woods inside. 'Please let it snow for Sita this Christmas,' she whispered quietly. The globe lit up brightly for a second and Lucy felt a tingling excitement run through her. Was it her imagination or could she hear tinkling sleigh bells? Lucy felt a little Christmassy flutter of happiness.

'Goodnight Lucy—I can't wait to explore tomorrow morning! I think this Christmas is going to be so much fun!' said Sita.

'I do too,' said Lucy, and glanced over at the snow globe. 'And maybe a little magical too,' she said hopefully to herself, as she drifted off to sleep.

Christmas wishes really can come true with Lucy!

ANNE BOOTH

Can Lucy make Starlight better and save Christmas?

Lucy's Secret REINDEER

Illustrated by Sophy Williams

ANNE BOOTH

Can Lucy save Christmas for a poorly rabbit?

Lucy's Magic SNOW GLOBE

Illustrated by Sophy Williams

ANNE BOOTH

Christmas miracles come in all sizes

Lucy's Winter RESCUE

Illustrated by Sophy Williams

Here are some other stories we think you'll love!